Billy and Fatcat were on their way to a fancy-dress party.
Fatcat wasn't that keen on dressing up, but Billy promised
him there would be cake.

The party was
in full swing.

They said
hello
to Fox . . .

Hello to Hedgehog . . .

Hello to the mice . . .

And hello to the adorable little bunny rabbits.

Fatcat quickly made his way to the snack table.

He was just about to tuck into a delicious sticky bun when . . .

Something big and mysterious swooped down from the sky . . .

and grabbed Fatcat!

"That looked like a massive dragon!" said Fox.
"Yes," agreed Hedgehog. "It definitely seemed dragony.
And it's taking Fatcat to the Deep Dark Forest, which
is full of savage creatures and mysterious dangers!"
"Hey!" shouted Billy. "Come back!"
But the dragon wasn't coming back.

Billy had to think fast . . .

She rummaged in her hair,
where she kept useful things . . .

and found a telescope!

Eventually she spotted Fatcat.
He had been plonked high up
in a tall tree and didn't seem
too happy about it.

"We've got to save Fatcat!" said Billy. "Who's with me?"
"We are!" said the mice.
"We are!" said the adorable little bunny rabbits.
"I suppose so . . ." said Hedgehog.
"Well . . . I have to say yes now, don't I?" said Fox.

But
when
they
got
to
the
Deep
Dark
Forest,
the
tree
was
too
big
to
climb.

How on earth was Billy going to get up there?

But Billy had an idea.

She held on to as many balloons as she could manage . . .

It was
working!

and higher . . .

higher . . .

and started to float . . .

POP!

POP!

POP!

Until the fearsome
dragon's roar popped
the balloons in an instant!

Billy plummeted to the ground . . .

. . . and

landed

with

a

most

fortunate

BOUNCE.

Phew.

But the dragon wasn't hanging around.
It grabbed Fatcat firmly in its claws
and flew even further away.

"Oh no! It's taken Fatcat to the Grimbly Mountains!"
gasped Hedgehog.
"They are full of even more savage creatures
and mysterious dangers!"

"Oh, what a shame," said Fox.
"He was a such nice cat. Who's for trifle?"

But Billy had no time for pudding.

She set off, all on her own.

The journey was indeed full of dangers.
Billy scrambled over treacherous rocks . . .

Leapt over gushing waterfalls . . .

And made friends with savage creatures.

Suddenly, she heard a SKWALK!

It was a dragon. Quite a small one.

It reminded Billy of someone.
"Are you lost?" she asked.
"I think someone might be looking for you."

Billy popped the little dragon into her backpack
and clambered up the rocky mountainside.
She was almost at the top . . .

But the fearsome dragon
was waiting!

It was
about to breathe
a fiery roar over Billy . . .

. . . when the little dragon
popped out to say hello!

"Mama!"
said the baby dragon.
"Simon!"
said the mummy dragon.

"Fatcat!"
said Billy.

"Turns out it was
all just a silly mix-up!"
said a little worm
who nobody
had noticed
until now.

The dragon gave Billy
and Fatcat a ride back to the party.
Everyone was excited
to meet the new guests.

And the party carried on into the bright, black night.

For Samina x

JONATHAN CAPE

UK | USA | Canada | Ireland | Australia
India | New Zealand | South Africa
Jonathan Cape is part of the Penguin Random House
group of companies whose addresses can be found at
global.penguinrandomhouse.com.
www.penguin.co.uk
www.puffin.co.uk
www.ladybird.co.uk

Penguin
Random House
UK

First published 2019
001

Printed in China

A CIP catalogue record for this book is
available from the British Library

ISBN: 978–0–857–55135–1

All correspondence to:
Jonathan Cape, Penguin Random House Children's
80 Strand, London WC2R 0RL

NADIA SHIREEN

BILLY
AND THE
DRAGON

JONATHAN CAPE · LONDON